A Very Naughty Little Girl

by

Abigail Strauss

Illustrations by Su Novis

Grosvenor House
Publishing Limited

This book is published by
Grosvenor House Publishing Ltd
Link House
140 The Broadway, Tolworth, Surrey, KT6 7HT.
www.grosvenorhousepublishing.co.uk

This book is a work of fiction. Any resemblance to
people or events, past or present, is purely coincidental.

A CIP record for this book
is available from the British Library

ISBN 978-1-83975-428-9

ACKNOWLEDGEMENTS

This book would not have been possible without the invaluable support and encouragement of my sister and best friend, Julie. Her enthusiasm inspired me to write this book, for which I will be eternally grateful.

My gratitude also goes to my lifelong friend, Su Novis, whose charming illustrations have brought my book to life.

CHAPTER ONE

Jennifer opened the attic door a few inches and two pairs of glass eyes gazed back at her. "Oh, you poor darlings, at last I've found you!" cried Jennifer.

The attic was used for storing things that were not used very often and was very dusty – it was a horrible place for her favourite teddy bears to be hidden.

Jennifer had been searching for her teddies all over the house for hours. She knew who the culprit was because this unkind prank had happened before; it was her best friend, Sarah, who had come to play. Sometimes Sarah was very naughty and could do and say mean things.

CHAPTER TWO

The two girls first met at nursery, they were now both six years old and in the same class at school. In spite of Sarah's bouts of bad behaviour, the pair were inseparable.

Cuddling her two teddies and feeling hurt and angry, Jennifer went to find her so-called "best friend". Sarah was in the playroom watching television with a smug expression on her face. "How could you be so cruel!" screamed Jennifer. "I never do anything to hurt you, so why are you so mean to me?"

"Children, dinner's ready," called Jennifer's mother, Vicky. "It's your favourite – fish fingers and spaghetti hoops!"

"Thank you, Mrs Wells," said Sarah, politely.

"Now, what's all the shouting about; have you two been squabbling again?" asked Vicky sternly.

Jennifer was tempted to tell her mother what Sarah had done but was reluctant to do so because the promised sleepover that night might be cancelled as a punishment.

CHAPTER THREE

As the girls made their way upstairs for a bubble bath before bedtime, Sarah muttered, "Sorry."

Jennifer ignored her friend's apology as she was still upset and angry.

Vicky stood at the bathroom door watching the girls who were unusually quiet and thought, "Something is seriously wrong between these two."

Jennifer's daddy, Charlie, arrived home from work in time to read the girls a bedtime story. He called out to his wife, "Hi darling, I'm home! Just going to say goodnight to the girls." He bounded up the stairs and when he reached his daughter's bedroom, he instantly sensed an atmosphere – something was not right between the two friends. Charlie sat on the side of the bed and said, "OK, what's happened?" The girls sat in silence. Suddenly, there was a shriek and a loud crash from downstairs. Charlie raced from the bedroom with the children close behind him. As they clambered down the stairs, Charlie shouted, "Are you OK, Vicky?" When they reached the kitchen they found Vicky on the floor surrounded by a smashed casserole dish and its contents all over the place.

"I'm alright – just a bit bruised. I slipped when taking our dinner out of the oven."

"Don't worry dear, as long as you are not hurt. We'll treat ourselves to a takeaway," he said, as he helped her up from the floor. "Come on girls, help me clear this mess up and then I'll make us all a nice hot chocolate."

The shock of what had happened to her mother brought Jennifer to her senses, as she realised that the accident could have been much worse and was far more important than her petty quarrel with Sarah. She decided to forgive Sarah but made her promise not to do anything like it again. As the girls were drifting off to sleep Sarah murmured, "I really will try to be a nicer friend."

CHAPTER FOUR

Sarah loved coming to play at Jennifer's house because it was big and old with lots of nooks and crannies to crawl into whenever the girls played hide and seek. Jennifer and Sarah's parents were also great friends and both families often got together for a barbeque or a picnic in the park where they played rounders. Between the two families there were enough members to make two good teams with Sarah's mummy Danielle, her daddy Tim and her four brothers, Mat, Nick, Lee and Zane. Her brother Zane was the eldest, but she hadn't seen him for ages as he'd been away at university.

CHAPTER FIVE

The day after the sleepover, Jennifer and Sarah were back at school, following the half term break, and both girls were looking forward to seeing their classmates again. The little group of friends met in the playground, chattering excitedly. The other members of the gang, Isabella, Maya, Thea and Justine, were all in the same class as Jennifer and Sarah and they loved their teacher, Janine, who always had time to listen.

CHAPTER SIX

In the house next door to Jennifer lived a lovely lady called Julie who had a parrot called Dora. "Julie's parrot can talk!" explained Jennifer to Sarah, "and when you speak to it the parrot copies what you say. It sounds just like your own voice!" she laughed. "Dora is a very pretty parrot with lovely brightly coloured feathers," she added.

"I think Dora is a very odd name for a bird," replied Sarah nastily.

"There you go again; you just can't help being MEAN can you?" shouted Jennifer.

"Okay, okay," said Sarah, and then she tried to make amends by saying, "Have your favourite teddy bears got names?"

"Yes, but I'm not telling you what they are because it will give you an excuse to be nasty again," snapped Jennifer.

"No, I won't, I promise," cried Sarah.

"Alright, but don't you dare be unkind," warned Jennifer. "Their names are Daisy and Henry."

Sarah clapped her hands and said sweetly, "Ooh what beautiful names."

"Well, well, things are looking up!" thought Jennifer.

CHAPTER SEVEN

The neighbour on the other side of Jennifer's house was also a friend of the family and happened to be a piano teacher called Maisie-Jean. She was a kind lady and Jennifer enjoyed her weekly piano lessons, after which she was rewarded with a sweet or a piece of chocolate.

It was a friendly road where Jennifer lived and everyone knew everyone. The teenage brother and sister who lived opposite often came over to babysit when Jennifer's parents went out. She looked forward to these times because being an only child could be lonely, so when Lotte and Oliver came to babysit they always played a game with her like cards or they did a puzzle.

CHAPTER EIGHT

Today, Sarah was looking forward to her eldest brother, Zane, finally coming home for the weekend as she was very fond of him. In the meantime, she decided to tease her other brothers and hide their football while they were busy on their phones. Out in the garden the family's pet dog, Rusty, was playing with a football. The loveable, bouncy, crossbred terrier, Rusty, had been with the family since she was a puppy. She came from a local rescue home for dogs.

Sarah grabbed the football and wondered where she could hide it but then thought of the perfect place. There was a long, low cupboard under the stairs where the football would be out of sight if it was rolled into a corner right at the back.

CHAPTER NINE

Danielle called to the boys, "Turn off your phones now and go and get some fresh air before dinner."

"Oh, must we?" whined Nick.

"Come on, let's play footie!" shouted Mat.

The boys searched the garden but couldn't find the football. "Mum," said Lee, "Have you seen our football?"

"It was by the goalpost last time I saw it," she replied. "I'm too busy to help you look now, the others will be here soon."

Sarah sat quietly watching television with a guilty smile on her face.

Jennifer's family had been invited to join them for dinner and suddenly there was pandemonium as everyone arrived together. Seated round the large dining table, they were all talking at once and enjoyed the delicious roast dinner followed by strawberries and cream.

CHAPTER TEN

There was a hush as everyone tucked in and then Mat announced, "A very strange thing happened today – our football has disappeared."

"We've searched everywhere – it's a complete mystery," said Lee. Suddenly everyone went quiet. They all turned their heads slowly to gaze at Sarah.

"I don't believe it," shrieked Jennifer; "after all your promises!"

Sarah blushed bright red and was obviously guilty.

"They all hate me," thought Sarah miserably. "I have to get away from all those accusing looks." Head bowed, she slid off her chair and ran out of the room and ran and ran and ran…

"Come back Sarah, let's talk about this," called Tim.

But Sarah was already out of earshot, her cheeks wet with tears, not knowing where to go.

"I expect she will be back in no time full of apologies," suggested Zane.

"I think we should give her twenty minutes and then we should all go and look for her," responded Danielle.

Everyone murmured their agreement.

CHAPTER ELEVEN

"Right," said Charlie, jumping up from the table, "Time's up."

"Let's start in the garden," said Danielle.

It was a lovely big garden with lots of places to hide so they spread out in all directions and searched the Wendy house, the greenhouse, the tool shed and the garage. Nothing.

Standing in the middle of the lawn, they were all talking at once deciding what to do next. Sarah's brothers all agreed their sister was too sensible to stray far from her home. Vicky said she would check with the neighbours. The houses on both sides and the family opposite were Sarah's friends.

CHAPTER TWELVE

"We haven't searched the house yet," pointed out Nick.

"Well, what are we waiting for, let's go!" shouted Lee.

A while later, everyone gathered again with gloomy faces. "Do you think we should call the police?" asked Mat.

"We'll wait another half an hour and then I'll ring them," said Tim.

Out in the road, Maisie-Jean, Julie, Lotte and Oliver had gathered to help. Other neighbours were coming out to join the search. Tim was just about to pick up the phone to call the police when Jennifer shouted, "WAIT, did anybody check the attic?"

No one had.

CHAPTER THIRTEEN

There was great excitement as they all scrambled up the stairs to the top floor with Jennifer in the lead. She saw the door to the attic was slightly open so she gently opened it a little further. As she peered inside two teary blue eyes gazed back at her, which made Jennifer begin to cry. She threw the door open and hauled her friend out, hugging her at the same time.

Sarah whispered to Jennifer, "I'm sorry for those things I did, I was angry when Zane went away and I was mean to you."

There was a cacophony of noise as everyone was laughing, crying, shouting and talking excitedly. Nick yelled, "Three cheers for Sarah; that's the best game of hide-and-seek I've ever played!"

"Hip hip hooray, hip hip hooray, hip hip hooray!" they chorused.

And so, the day ended happily as the families descended the stairs from the attic and went into the garden where they sat in the sun and enjoyed ice cream cones.

Jennifer whispered to her best friend, "I do love a story that has a happy ending."

THE END